W9-ACO-197

11/2019

DISCARD

Fall Colors

Written by Margo Gates

Illustrated by Brian Hartley

GRL Consultants, Diane Craig and Monica Marx,
Certified Literacy Specialists

Lerner Publications ◆ Minneapolis

Note from a GRL Consultant
This Pull Ahead leveled book has been carefully designed for beginning readers. A team of guided reading literacy experts has reviewed and leveled the book to ensure readers pull ahead and experience success.

Lerner Publications Company
A division of Lerner Publishing Group, Inc.
241 First Avenue North
Minneapolis, MN 55401 USA

For reading levels and more information, look up this title at www.lernerbooks.com.

Main body text set in Mikado 24/41
Typeface provided by Hannes von Doehren.

The images in this book are used with the permission of: Brian Hartley.

Library of Congress Cataloging-in-Publication Data

Names: Gates, Margo, author. | Hartley, Brian, illustrator.
Title: Fall colors / by Margo Gates ; illustrated by Brian Hartley.
Description: Minneapolis : Lerner Publications, [2020] | Series: Seasons all around me (Pull ahead readers - Fiction) | Includes index.
Identifiers: LCCN 2018056966 (print) | LCCN 2018057753 (ebook) | ISBN 9781541562400 (eb pdf) | ISBN 9781541558748 (lb : alk. paper) | ISBN 9781541573413 (pb : alk. paper)
Subjects: LCSH: Readers (Primary) | Colors—Juvenile fiction. | Autumn—Juvenile fiction. | Asian Americans—Juvenile fiction.
Classification: LCC PE1119 (ebook) | LCC PE1119 .G38425 2020 (print) | DDC 428.6/2—dc23

LC record available at https://lccn.loc.gov/2018056966

Manufactured in the United States of America
1 – CG – 7/15/19

Contents

Fall Colors 4

Did You See It? 16

Index 16

Fall Colors

Fall has many colors.
Sam looked for the
color red.
"The apples are red,"
he said.

Sam looked for the color yellow.
"The leaves are yellow," he said.

Sam looked for the
color orange.
"The pumpkins are orange,"
he said.

Sam looked for the color green.
"The grass is green," he said.

Sam looked for the
color blue.
"The sky is blue,"
he said.

Sam looked for the color brown.
"Maya's fur is brown!" he said.

Did You See It?

apples

dog

grass

leaves

pumpkins

sky

Index

apples, 4
blue, 12
brown, 14
fur, 14

grass, 10
green, 10
leaves, 6
Maya, 14
orange, 8

pumpkins, 8
red, 4
sky, 12
yellow, 6